World of Reading

LEVEL 1

THIS IS SPIDER-MAN

Adapted by **Thomas Macri**
Illustrated by **Todd Nauck** and **Hi-Fi Design**
Based on the Marvel comic book series **Spider-Man**

New York • Los Angeles

D0032906

marvelkids.com

© 2012 MARVEL

Printed in the United States of America

First Edition

15 17 19 20 18 16

FAC-029261-20016

ISBN 978-1-4231-5408-2

SUSTAINABLE FORESTRY INITIATIVE

Certified Chain of Custody
Promoting Sustainable Forestry

www.sfiprogram.org
SFI-01415

The SFI label applies to the text stock

This is Peter.

Peter lives in Queens.
Queens is in
New York City.

Peter lives with his aunt.
Her name is Aunt May.

Peter loves Aunt May
very much.

Peter is a student.

He goes to high school.

Peter loves school.
He loves math.

He loves science.

Some kids at school are
not nice to Peter.

They push him.
They make fun of him.

Peter does not care.

At home, no one makes fun
of Peter.

Peter has a super secret.

He has a costume.

He has web-shooters.

He makes webs.

He shoots webs.

This is his costume.
It has a spider on it.
It has webs on it, too.

Peter puts on his costume.
Peter has a secret name.

He calls himself
Spider-Man.

This is Spider-Man.

Spider-Man can climb
up walls.

He can swing on
his webs.

He shoots his webs.

His webs stop bad guys.

Peter takes off his mask.
He is tired.

Peter goes to sleep.

Peter wakes up. He gets
ready for school.

At school, the kids learn
about Spider-Man.

They like Spider-Man.

They do not like Peter.

But they do not know
Peter's secret.

Peter is Spider-Man.